W9-DCL-415
02/2017

PALM BEACH COUNTY
LIBRARY SYSTEM
3650 Summit Boulevard
West Palm Beach, FL 33406-4198

Margaret Hillert's

Away Go the Boats

A Beginning-to-Read Book

Illustrated by Kathie Kelleher

DEAR CAREGIVER,

The books in this Beginning-to-Read collection may look somewhat familiar in that the original versions could have been a part of your own early reading experiences. These carefully written texts feature common sight words to provide your child multiple exposures to the words appearing most frequently in written text. These new versions have been updated and the engaging illustrations are highly appealing to a contemporary audience of young readers.

Begin by reading the story to your child, followed by letting him or her read familiar words and soon your child will be able to read the story independently. At each step of the way, be sure to praise your reader's efforts to build his or her confidence as an independent reader. Discuss the pictures and encourage your child to make connections between the story and his or her own life. At the end of the story, you will find reading activities and a word list that will help your child practice and strengthen beginning reading skills. These activities, along with the comprehension questions are aligned to current standards, so reading efforts at home will directly support the instructional goals in the classroom.

Above all, the most important part of the reading experience is to have fun and enjoy it!

Shannon Cannon

Shannon Cannon,
Literacy Consultant

Norwood House Press • www.norwoodhousepress.com
Beginning-to-Read™ is a registered trademark of Norwood House Press.
Illustration and cover design copyright ©2017 by Norwood House Press. All Rights Reserved.

Authorized adapted reprint from the U.S. English language edition, entitled Away Go the Boats by Margaret Hillert. Copyright © 2017 Margaret Hillert. Reprinted with permission. All rights reserved. Pearson and Away Go the Boats are trademarks, in the US and/or other countries, of Pearson Education, Inc. or its affiliates. This publication is protected by copyright, and prior permission to re-use in any way in any format is required by both Norwood House Press and Pearson Education. This book is authorized in the United States for use in schools and public libraries..

Designer: Lindaanne Donohoe
Editorial Production: Lisa Walsh

LIBRARY OF CONGRESS CATALOGING-IN-PUBLICATION DATA
Names: Hillert, Margaret, author. I Kelleher, Kathie, illustrator.
Title: Away go the boats / by Margaret Hillert ; illustrated by Kathie Kelleher.
Description: Chicago, IL : Norwood House Press, [2016] I Series: A Beginning-to-Read book I Originally published in 1981 by Follett Publishing Company. I Summary: During her bath a young girl takes an imaginary ocean voyage to a tropical island.
Identifiers: LCCN 2016001842 (print) I LCCN 2016022100 (ebook) I ISBN 9781599537924 (library edition : alk. paper) I ISBN 9781603579544 (eBook)
Subjects: I CYAC: Baths--Fiction. I Imagination--Fiction.
Classification: LCC PZ7.H558 Aw 2016 (print) I LCC PZ7.H558 (ebook) I DDC [E]--dc23
LC record available at https://lccn.loc.gov/2016001842

288N—072016
Manufactured in the United States of America in North Mankato, Minnesota.

Mother said, "Come on now.
I want you to get in here.
Get in. Get in."

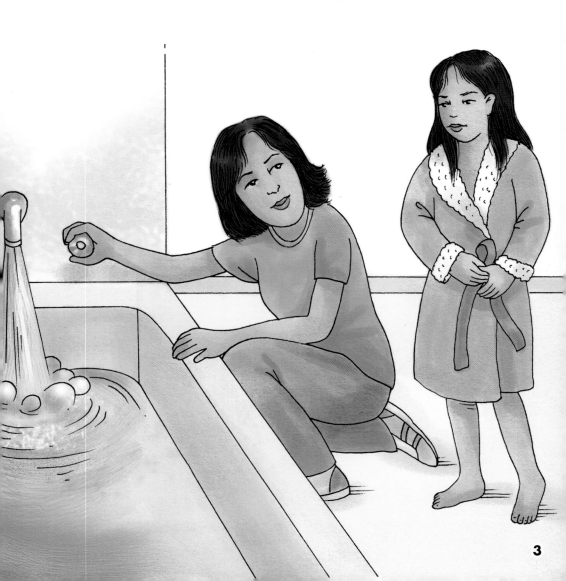

The girl said, "Do I have to?
I do not want to.
I want to play."

4

Mother said, "Yes, yes.
Here is something for
you to play with.
Here is a boat.
A little blue boat."

"Oh, good," said the girl.
"My little blue boat.
 I like this boat.
 It is fun to play with."

Mother said, "Jump in.
Jump in, and I will go.
I have work to do.
You have work to do, too.
Do it. Do it."

"This is a good, good boat.
   Go, boat, go.
   Go, go, go."

Now I will play that this boat
is a big one.
I will get on it.
I will go away, away.

Here I am on my big boat.
I can make it go
where I want it to go.

Where will I go?
What will I find?
What will I see?

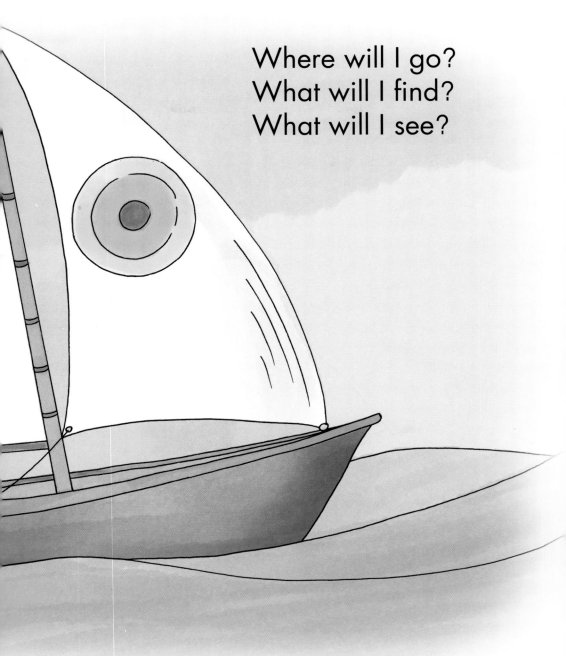

Look, look.
I see the sun.
I see three boats too.
One, two, three boats.
Away go the boats.

And away I go, too.
On and on I go.
What fun!
What fun!

Look up.
Up, up, up.
Way, way up.
Look what I see.

Now look at that.
How big it is.
Big, big, big.
How it can jump!

Here is a good spot.
I can get out here.
I can look for something.

Oh, who are you?
My, you are a pretty one.
Yellow, blue and green.

And look here.
Oh, what do I see here?
One, two, three little ones.
Three funny little ones.

Oh, oh!
You are not funny.
You are too big for me.
I guess I will go away now.

22

Here I go.
Away, away.
What a good ride this is!

"Oh, Mother.
Do I have to get out now?
I like it here.
It is fun."

"Yes, yes.
Get out. Get out.
Come out now.
I will help you."

"I will get out, but I will
take the boat with me.
It is a good little boat."

Foundational Skills

In addition to reading the numerous high-frequency words in the text, this book also supports the development of foundational skills.

Phonological Awareness: Phonogram -ay

Oral Blending: Say the beginning sounds and word endings below for your child. Ask your child to say the new word made by blending the beginning and ending word parts together:

/b/ + ay = bay	/m/ + ay = may	/tr/ + ay = tray
/r/ + ay = ray	/p/ + ay = pay	/h/ + ay = hay
/w/ + ay = way	/pl/ + ay = play	/s/ + ay = say
/d/ + ay = day	/l/ + ay = lay	/gr/ + ay = gray
/st/ + ay = stay	/cl/ + ay = clay	

Phonics: Phonogram -ay

1. Write the following phonogram (word ending) ten times in a row on a piece of paper: __**ay**
2. For each row, help your child write a letter (or letters) in the blank to make a word. If you have letter tiles, or magnetic letters, it may help your child to move the letter into the space.
3. Ask your child to read the rhyming words.

Fluency: Echo Reading

1. Reread the story to your child at least two more times while your child tracks the print by running a finger under the words as they are read. Ask your child to read the words he or she knows with you.
2. Reread the story, stopping after each sentence or page to allow your child to read (echo) what you have read. Repeat echo reading and let your child take the lead.

Language

The concepts, illustrations, and text in this book help children develop language both explicitly and implicitly.

Vocabulary: Story-Related Words

1. Write the following words on sticky note paper and point to them as you read them to your child:

   seagulls   dolphins   parrot   monkeys   lion

2. Mix the words up. Say each word in random order and ask your child to point to the correct word as you say it.
3. Mix the words up and ask your child to read as many as he or she can.
4. Ask your child to place the sticky notes on the correct page for each word that describes something in the story.
5. Say the following sentences aloud and ask your child to point to the word that is described:

   • The girl looked up to see the _____ flying above her. (seagulls)

   • The _____ jumped out of the water. (dolphins)

   • She thought the _____ was pretty. (parrot)

   • On the island, she saw _____ climbing in the trees. (monkeys)

   • When she saw the _____ she decided it was time to go home. (lion)

Reading Literature and Informational Text

To support comprehension, ask your child the following questions. The answers either come directly from the text or require inferences and discussion.

Key Ideas and Detail

• Ask your child to retell the sequence of events in the story.
• Did the girl actually ride in a sailboat?

Craft and Structure

• Is this a book that tells a story or one that gives information? How do you know?
• Why do you think the mother wanted the girl to hurry to get in the bath?

Integration of Knowledge and Ideas

• Using your imagination: if you had a boat, where would you like to go?
• What tools did the girl use on the boat to help her find her way?

Away Go the Boats uses the 73 words listed below.

This list can be used to practice reading the words that appear in the text. You may wish to write the words on index cards and use them to help your child build automatic word recognition. Regular practice with these words will enhance your child's fluency in reading connected text.

a	get	like	ride	want
am	girl	little		way
and	go	look	said	what
are	good		see	where
at	green	make	something	who
away	guess	me	spot	will
		Mother	sun	with
big	have	my		work
blue	help		take	
boat(s)	here	not	that	yellow
but	how	now	the	yes
			this	you
can	I	oh	three	
come	in	on	to	
	is	one(s)	too	
do	it	out	two	
find	jump	play	up	
for		pretty		
fun				
funny				

ABOUT THE AUTHOR Margaret Hillert has helped millions of children all over the world learn to read independently. She was a first grade teacher for 34 years and during that time started writing books that her students could both gain confidence in reading and enjoy. She wrote well over 100 books for children just learning to read. As a child, she enjoyed writing poetry and continued her poetic writings as an adult for both children and adults.

Photograph by Glenna Washburn

ABOUT THE ILLUSTRATOR A graduate of Paier College of Art, Kathie Kelleher has illustrated for numerous publishers. Specializing in educational art while raising her two daughters, Kathie's transition into the world of picture books was met with much success. She recently realized a life-long dream of writing her own children's book. www.kathiekelleher.com